BURDENS OF HOPE

BURDENS OF HOPE

LEGENDS OF LYORION

THE HOPEBRINGER TRILOGY

A COMPANION NOVELLA

DAVID DUNFEE

TABLE OF CONTENTS

FOR EVERY SOUL CARRYING UNSEEN BURDENS.
MAY THEY KNOW THEY WERE NEVER MEANT TO CARRY THEM ALONE.

A SPOON'S BURDEN

SPOONY

"The man who brought the beast down wasn't the only one changed that night."

I let the spoon turn once through my fingers before catching it against the table.

Several of the patrons leaned in, eager to get started.

"Most folk prefer the polished telling. Goes down smoother," I said.

The ones who weren't familiar with the Spoon Inn learned quickly enough once the story started.

"Lightning in the sky. Man on the tower. Hammer in hand. Beast on the ground."

I gave a small shrug.

"Makes for a fine end to an evening. Gives them something grand to cheer for before they stumble home happy."

The spoon slipped beneath the cover.

"Everything after that has a habit of being left behind. The lives underneath it most of all."

The cover flipped open in one motion.

"So, I went looking for what got left behind."

I glanced around the room once more, making sure they were still with me.

"Name's Spoony."

The spoon settled on the first line.

"These are the Burdens of Hope."

CHAPTER I: THE FESTIVAL

MIRA

Sapphire and crimson light blossomed above Fall Lake, their reflections dancing across the dark water in ribbons of light. Mira Vale lifted her hand toward the sky without thinking, and there it was again, the silver band wrapped around her finger, catching the burst of color as if it had stolen a piece of the celebrations for itself.

She could not help but smile at it, her thumb brushing the edge of the ring as it caught the light.

Again.

For what was likely the thousandth time.

Tomas let out a soft laugh beside her. "You know, love, if you keep staring at that ring every few breaths, folk are going to think you only married me for the jewelry."

Mira's smile widened as she looked at her new husband. "And what if I only married you for it?"

"That would be cruel. Accurate, perhaps, but cruel."

She laughed and leaned into him, his arm already settling around her waist.

One week since the vows. One week since Tomas had fumbled the ring only once and looked so horrified by it that she had nearly laughed aloud at the altar. One week since her mother had cried harder than she had.

One week since they had promised each other a life neither of them could fully picture yet, only that they wanted it together.

She had worn the ring proudly, but it still felt strange and wonderful each time she caught sight of it, as if the world had shifted beneath her feet and left her standing in a better one than before.

Another firework burst above them, this one gold at its heart before spilling into white sparks that drew a chorus of cheers from the gathered crowd. Music rolled through the streets beneath, flutes and drums and handclaps weaving together with laughter, shouted greetings, and the calls of merchants still trying to wring a few final sales from festivalgoers too full and happy to resist.

The whole of Fall Lake was alive in a way Mira had never seen before.

She lifted her eyes higher, past the fireworks and smoke, toward the joined glow of the twin moons above.

Luna's smaller shape had long since disappeared behind Mani's broader face, leaving the sky washed in that strange violet hue that only came during Lunamani. Luna's softer blue. Mani's warmer red. When they crossed, their light bled together into a purple sheen.

Mira always loved that.

Lunamani came twice each year, but this was the greater turning. The one people traveled for. This was the one children remembered. And sweethearts made promises beneath, hoping the sky would help keep them.

The old year ended beneath Mani's shadow and the new one began there.

It had felt right to begin their life beneath it.

This year, Fall Lake had more reason than most to celebrate.

Lanterns hung in bright rows between rooftops and raised posts, with colored glass swaying gently in the night breeze rolling in off the water. Newly built stalls lined the main road beside stonework and half-finished corners of a city still growing into itself. Ribbons of festival blue and gold had been tied to railings, archways, market posts, and dock beams until the streets looked dressed for the Zenarian royalty. People filled every open stretch of freshly paved road.

Fall Lake had once been little more than a hardworking fishing settlement with a good harbor and stubborn people. Now it shimmered with the pride of something becoming much more. New homes rose where old lots had once sat empty. Storehouses and workshops had spread farther inland. Roads had been widened. Stone had begun replacing what wood alone could no longer carry. The city still smelled of lakewater and fish in many corners, but now it carried the scent of mortar, sawdust, and ambition too.

The rough edges of the new capital no longer felt unfinished. They felt full of possibility.

Humans filled most of the roads, but Mira spotted the Nogmi easily enough, loud as ever and impossible to miss, their stalls brighter, stranger, and busier than most. Dwarv stood in smaller knots this year, broad-shouldered and watchful, more subdued than the festival usually called for. They seemed more on guard than usual, rather than given over to drinking, smoking, and provocative activities they were more known for. Their change in demeanor was something both Mira and Tomas noticed. There used to be more of them.

She didn't say it aloud.

Most people with any sense kept their tongues careful this week regarding the matter.

The old wounds between the people of Shularix were never as far beneath the skin as folk liked to pretend, and the absence of their larger numbers sat in the crowd like an unspoken bruise. Still, those who had come were here beneath the same purple sky as everyone else, taking part in the same week meant to quiet pride, settle grudges, and remind the world that peace was not a foolish dream simply because it was difficult.

Tomas had drifted half a step nearer without saying anything, not enough to crowd her, only enough that she felt him there between her and the thickest part of the road. He did that sometimes when the streets got busy, never making a show of it. Just quietly making space where he could.

The Elfar were here too, though fewer than Mira remembered from the first days of the festival.

For one blessed week, borders opened.

Trade softened suspicion. Music covered old divisions well enough to let people breathe.

Mira breathed it in, her chest filling with something she could not quite place.

Just ahead, near the edge of the lane, a line of festival lanterns had come loose where it had been tied between a post and the corner of a stall. One side sagged low enough that taller folk were ducking beneath it as they passed. A man carrying a crate stepped out of the crowd, set his burden down without a word, and climbed onto the side rail of the stall.

His hands moved quickly. He retied the line, gave the knot a firm pull to test it, adjusted the lean of one crooked lantern beside it, then hopped back down as if the whole thing had been nothing worth noticing.

Mira watched him lift the crate again and disappear into the moving sea of people. She would remember him later, though she didn't know why.

"Good man," Tomas said, watching him disappear into the crowd.

She smiled. "There are still some."

The roasted sweetness of sugared nuts drifted from one stall. A sharper scent of smoked riverfish lingered near the docks. Somewhere behind them, a vendor was shouting about spiced honeycakes. Farther down the lane, a Nogmi man stood atop a crate, waving a skewer of something glazed and steaming while insisting at full volume that no sensible person should leave the festival without trying it at least once.

"Even if you breathe fire afterwards," he shouted.

That only made the crowd around him laugh harder.

Tomas tipped his chin toward the shouting vendor. "That one. You said you wanted something different from each of the people before the night ended."

Mira squinted as she watched one person actually cough a spark after claiming one of the skewers. "That… is food, I suppose."

"You say that as though food is not a gift from the gods."

"True, but it's not a keepsake we can put in *our* home." She emphasized the words as she pressed herself comfortably into her new husband.

"It can be, if you remember it fondly enough. Maybe we can find a street artist to paint a picture of us eating it."

She gave him a dry look that failed her the moment his smile warmed her. "I meant something we could keep. A charm. A carving. A piece of each place. Each culture. Something to remember this night and this week by."

Tomas touched the gleaming ring on her finger. "Was this not enough for you? This took my entire life savings."

"It is enough," she said softly, her smile warming. "But this is ours. I want something from the rest too, while it's here."

"The rest?"

"The rest of the world." She gestured with her free hand toward the crowd, the lights, the music, the color all around them. Her fingers lingered in the air as if trying to hold it all there. "All of this. Look at it."

Tomas did look, properly this time, and she saw the same thing in him that had first made them bold enough to come.

Not certainty. No one had that in a city still smelling of fresh construction. What they had was promise.

Fall Lake was young enough that people like them could still claim a corner of it and call it theirs. Tomas could build while she made their home here. They would not spend their lives buried beneath the shadow of older families and older streets where every future had already been spoken for.

Here, it still felt unwritten.

And in his eyes, she saw it too. Not safety exactly, but the quiet, stubborn belief that something better might still be made if enough people chose it.

Tomas nodded slowly. "All right. One keepsake from each people. But only if you accept that I may make a bad choice."

"You do tend to choose badly."

"And yet you married me."

"That may be my poorest choice."

He pressed a hand to his chest as though mortally wounded.

"And after I married you, too!"

Mira brushed her shoulder against his as she spoke. "And still you stay."

His mouth twitched. "Against all reason."

"A poor habit to begin a marriage with."

That got a real laugh out of him, the kind that pulled one from her in return before she could stop herself.

A small girl darted between them and nearly caught herself in Mira's skirt, paper ribbons tied in her hair and sugar shining at the corner of her mouth. A breathless older woman swooped in after her, apologizing while the girl giggled and twisted free just enough to point excitedly toward the docks where another row of fireworks was being readied.

The next firework let out a massive roar of sparks and curling flame, loud enough to tremble through the stones beneath them. Mira laughed under her breath and tipped her face up to it like she had when she was little. They had never done them this grand.

"Sorry," the woman said again through her own smiles, "She's decided sleep is for the weak."

"She sounds wise," Tomas said.

The woman snorted and hurried on after the child.

Mira watched them longer than she needed to, until they were swallowed completely by the crowd. "I want that someday."

Tomas glanced at her. "A child who runs headfirst into strangers and festival carts?"

"You know what I mean."

His expression softened at once. "I do."

The answer was simple, but it settled warmly in her chest beside the weight of the ring.

Between shared meals, unpacked crates, and the strange joy of waking each morning and remembering they no longer belonged to separate futures.

A home with enough light for plants in the window.

A table that stayed too small because guests were always welcome.

A child with Tomas's smile and her stubbornness, or perhaps the other way around if the gods were feeling cruel.

One day.

Not yet. Not tonight.

But soon, she hoped.

That was what Fall Lake felt made of to her. Stone and sweat and lakewater, yes, but something brighter beneath it all too. *Hope,* stubborn and bright, tucked into every beam and promise.

They moved on, hand in hand.

At a Dwarv table, hammered bracelets lined a velvet cloth in neat rows, each one etched with tiny knotted waves and mountain marks worked so finely Mira had to lean close to admire its true beauty.

The Dwarv woman behind the display wore her hair braided tightly with metal rings and offered Mira a polite smile, though there was a reserve to it.

"They're beautiful," Mira said.

The woman nodded once. "Made by different members of the clan."

Tomas picked one up, turning it carefully in his hand. "You could wear this one. It would look good with the ring."

Mira smiled. "Or I could let you have one good choice this evening and save my criticism for later."

The woman huffed a quiet laugh at that, enough to lighten the exhaustion from her face. Mira liked earning even that much from her.

She bought one.

Not because it was the first Dwarv thing she had seen, but because something about the craft of it felt honest.

A few stalls farther on, a pair of Nogmi brothers had suspended tiny glass stars and moons above their table, if you would call it a table. Each one was filled with colored powders that shifted when the lantern light struck them just right. One of the brothers insisted they were imbued with "a very minor and only occasionally dangerous blessing of wonder," which Tomas found convincing enough to buy one immediately.

"That is going to explode before we make it home," Mira warned.

"But it could just sparkle instead," Tomas corrected.

"It may explode while sparkling," another Nogmi popped out from beneath the stall to add helpfully, or so he seemed to think.

"See, love, it could do both."

"Wife and widowed all within the same week," she laughed as he tucked the little glass star into a satchel.

A slower tune drifted over the road then, softer than the drums that had ruled the evening before it. Enough to make a few couples wander into the wider stretch between stalls and sway together beneath the lanterns.

Tomas glanced toward them.

Mira caught the look at once. "No."

His mouth opened. "I have not even asked."

"You were going to."

"I still might."

Her smile brightened in the lowered lantern light. "You dance like a man trying to escape with his life."

He pressed a hand to his chest. "That was one time."

"It was our wedding."

Tomas opened his mouth, no doubt to defend himself, but the slower tune drifting through the lane stole the words before they came. Mira followed the movements of the other couples without meaning to.

Tomas held out his hand.

This time, Mira did not say no.

"You'll step on me," she whispered without force as her hands slipped into place.

"Then I'll do it as your husband," he said gently. "That makes it romantic."

She laughed under her breath and let him draw her in closer.

He was not graceful. She had been right about that. Tomas moved like a man built more for hauling and lifting crates than gliding beneath moonlight, but he held her carefully, as though she were something precious enough to break if the world turned too quickly. One hand resting at the small of her back, the other closed around hers, and that alone was enough to make the rest of the festival fall away.

Mira let herself settle into the slow sway of it.

Music hummed, lanterns rocked in the breeze. Somewhere nearby, someone laughed too loudly over their mug, and another child shrieked in delight as another firework climbed into the heavens. But here, in Tomas's arms, she felt safe.

She felt home.

She rested her head against his chest, closing her eyes a second longer than needed. His heartbeat thudded warmly beneath her ear.

"Better than the wedding?"

"A little."

He smiled, and Mira didn't open her eyes to see it, but she felt it.

Her chest tightened with something so sudden and full it almost hurt. Not pain or fear. Just the unbearable weight of wanting a moment to last when she knew, even now, that moments like that never did.

She blinked, and to her own surprise felt a single tear slip free.

Tomas noticed at once. "Mira?"

She shook her head, smiling before he could worry. "Happy tears, I promise."

Happy didn't feel large enough for it. For the ring on her hand. For the city glowing around them. The strange beauty of the moons above. For the man holding her as if there was nowhere else in the world he would rather be.

She almost asked the moons, or Grace herself, to hold the moment still. To leave this one piece of her life untouched.

The thought came quiet as a breath, and left just as quickly. But it lingered enough for her to hold him tighter.

Tomas's thumb brushed over her knuckles. "Then stay here with me a little longer."

Mira shifted closer to him and followed his steps.

So they did.

They swayed there beneath Luna and Mani while the world sang around them, newlywed and full of the kind of aspiration only the young and unbroken ever believe can last. Mira let herself imagine it then, plainly and without shame. A home. A table. A child. Their life.

For a few precious breaths, it all seemed close enough to touch. Unlost. Unbroken.

Then the song ended, and the spell of it loosened just enough for the night to move again.

They still had one more keepsake to find.

And perhaps, time to go back for the fire-breathing skewers before the festival gave way to sleep.

By the time they reached the Elfar row, Mira had already begun scanning the displays. Earlier she had seen polished wood charms carved with leaf and curling patterns so delicate they looked like they might crumble beneath careless fingers. She had liked one in particular, a pendant shaped like a droplet with grain caught inside of it like frozen smoke.

She slowed where it once stood.

Now the stall was empty.

No vendor. No wares. No lantern burning beneath the awning.

Mira didn't move this time.

"It was here before."

Tomas looked over the booth, then stepped closer, one hand lightly at the small of her back.

"Maybe they sold out."

"Of everything?"

He opened his mouth, then paused.

The table had been cleared too neatly. No scraps of wrapping. No forgotten trinkets. No half-packed crates waiting to be hauled away. Even the cloth that had covered the display was gone, as though someone had decided the stall should leave no trace of itself behind.

Mira looked farther down the lane.

Another Elfar stall stood much the same. Bare table. Dark lantern. No sign of its owner. No voices. No movement.

Not abandoned.

Emptied.

As if they had been cleared out too quickly.

Something cold brushed over her skin despite the warmth of the crowd around them.

"Maybe they left early," Tomas said, though there was less certainty in his voice now. "Stay close."

"Maybe..." But the word sat wrong the moment it left her mouth, and the way Tomas had said stay close only made it worse.

Around them, the music still played. Laughter still rolled through the road. Children still tugged at sleeves and begged for sweets. Above it all, fireworks continued to paint the Lunamani sky in sapphire, crimson, gold, and white.

But something had shifted in the air, and she couldn't name it.

Just enough for Mira to have noticed.

Mira turned the ring once around her finger and forced herself to breathe. "Come on. We still need to find something before you convince me candied meat counts as culture and decor for our home."

"All right," he said. "One more pass, then we head home."

Mira nodded, though her eyes drifted once more toward the empty Elfar stalls before she let Tomas lead her on.

They had gone only a few paces when a sound rolled across Fall Lake that no firework could have made.

Deep. Inhuman.

Too vast for any living thing that belonged in the world of men.

The music faltered.

The crowd stilled.

Every smile in sight seemed to hesitate at once, as if the city had drawn in a single shared breath.

Then came a second sound.

Not a roar this time, but the crash of something enormous striking wood and stone.

A lantern post near the far end of the aisle shuddered. Heads turned. Voices lifted in confusion. Someone laughed nervously, too quickly and too loud, as if the noise might still be explained away by some drunken mishap or failed firework.

Then the roar came.

It split through the night like something tearing the world open.

A woman screamed.

Mira did not remember grabbing Tomas's arm, only that her nails were suddenly digging into his sleeve and every hair on her body had risen. The sound rolled through her chest hard enough that she felt the vibration in her teeth.

People began moving all at once.

Not running. Not yet.

Just the first ugly shuffle of nervousness. Bodies pressing together, moving before they knew where they meant to flee.

Questions thrown too quickly and answered by no one.

Hands grasping children and pulling them close.

"What was that?"

"Was it near the docks? I can't tell."

"No, I think it came from the north entrance."

"Another firework?"

"No."

"No, no, that was no firework."

A crash sounded again, louder this time, followed by splintering wooden planks and a fresh wave of screams somewhere deeper in the city.

This time the crowd broke.

Her eyes searched all around her.

Tomas pulled her close. "Stay with me."

She stayed where he pulled her, even as her eyes kept searching past him.

His words should have comforted the dread forming within her.

But they didn't. Not because of him. Because of how he had said them.

No teasing or warmth, only fear covered by protectiveness.

Festivalgoers surged down the lane toward them now, some crying, some shouting, some too breathless to do anything but shove through whoever stood in their way. A child went down near the center of the road. Mira leaned toward him before Tomas kept her with him. A man Mira had seen earlier hauled the boy upright by the back of his shirt just before he disappeared with the crowd.

A streak of blue fire burst above them, absurdly beautiful over a city whose joy had begun to crack.

Mira leaned forward despite the panicked crowd, searching past them toward the deeper streets of Fall Lake, where smoke had begun to rise in thick, gray curls against the joined light of Luna and Mani.

Beyond it, something roared again.

For the first time this week, the purple light above the city became witness to tragedy.

CHAPTER 2: THE BREAK

Jory

Jory Tiller thought the first roar was part of the fireworks.

It sounded wrong. Too big. Too deep. But the whole night had been noise already. Bursting colors. People shouting over one another. Drums he could feel in his chest. Marla crying because she wanted sweets, then crying because hers were gone before his were. Everything had been loud for so long that the sound only felt like one more thing piled onto the rest.

Then the grown-ups changed.

That was when he knew something was wrong.

His mother's hand clamped around his wrist so hard it hurt.

Not annoyed. Not distracted. Not the way she grabbed him when he wandered too close to carts or too near the lake.

Hard. Like if she let go, he would be gone forever.

Jory looked up at her. "Ma? You're hurting me."

She was staring over the heads around them, trying to see. Her mouth had gone tight. Marla had both fists bunched in her skirt and was already starting to whine again, upset because the fireworks had paused.

"Ma? Ma, wait—"

"Stay with me," she said.

That scared him more than the roar had.

Because mothers said things all kinds of ways. Angry. Tired. Busy. Laughing. This had not been any of those. She had said it like the words mattered more than anything else.

Another crash rolled somewhere across the city.

Not up in the sky. Not where fireworks belonged.

Something huge moved where no building should have moved.

It felt lower and closer to the ground. Like something huge had fallen over and broken everything beneath it.

People near them turned in different directions at once.

Their words all fell together until they stopped sounding like words at all.

Just noise. Too much noise. Too many mouths.

Their mother bent, grabbed Marla up with one arm, and hauled Jory closer with the other. "We're going back."

Back where, Jory did not know.

Home? The inn? Somewhere under a table maybe. Somewhere with walls. He did not ask because her voice was too strange and because the crowd was already starting to move before any of them understood why. Jory's sugar crusted fingers clung to his shirt when he tried to wipe them clean.

Then the roar came again.

This time it did not sound like fireworks.

This time it sounded like something alive.

The sound hit him so hard he forgot how to breathe.

Marla shrieked at the sound.

His mother swore and yanked both of them so hard Jory nearly lost his shoe. The road around them went crazy all at once. People were too close together. Elbows, backs, breaths, the smell of adult drinks that Jory had always hated.

Someone knocked into his shoulder hard enough to spin him halfway around. A man carrying a child shoved past, knocking another woman sideways. Somebody cried out that they were trampling people. Somebody else shouted back to keep moving.

Lanternlight swung above the road in wild circles.

"Move!"

"Which way?"

"Back!"

"No, not that way, you idiot!"

A little boy somewhere nearby started screaming for his father.

Jory grabbed harder at his mother's hand.

She was sweating.

He had never noticed his mother's hand sweat before.

That scared him too.

Something cracked overhead.

Jory looked up in time to see part of a painted festival arch split and buckle and something smashed through it. Bits of wood rained down. One sharp piece clipped a man in the forehead and he went down cursing. Before anyone helped him, others were already stepping over him, and onto his hand.

The road had stopped being a road.

It was only bodies now.

Too many legs.

Too many grown-ups.

Too many backs.

Too many shoes.

Too tall to see anything but people.

The sugar on his fingers and the sweat on his mother's hand made everything slippery.

Jory tried to stay close enough to his mother that his shoulder kept hitting her hip, but the crowd shoved from all sides. Marla was crying against their mother's shoulder. Jory could not even see her face anymore. He could only hear that broken little squeal she made when she was frightened enough to forget how to breathe between sobs.

"Jory, do not let go of me," their mother shouted.

He tried.

He really did.

He had her hand.

Then a shoulder hit him from behind. Someone stepped on the back of his shoe. It came off under the crowd and was gone.

His fingers slipped as he fumbled forward. He grabbed cloth. Lost it. Grabbed again.

And then his mother was gone.

He grabbed at the next sleeve he saw. Missed.

One heartbeat she had been there.

The next she was nowhere.

"Ma!"

He saw a skirt the right color and lunged for it. The woman turned and it was not her. A baby was tied against her chest, wailing at the chaos and panic. She shoved past him without even seeing him.

"Ma!"

A boot came down on his foot. Pain shot through his toes. He cried out and got swallowed by the shouting around him.

He could not see anything except coats and sleeves and hair and backs. But every time someone turned, their mouths were open too wide, wider than they should have been, and that scared him worse than the noise.

Marla was not there.

He no longer knew if Marla was holding onto his mother's shoulder.

Marla being alone was a thought he couldn't bear to consider.

"Marla! Ma!"

Nothing.

No answer.

Only people shouting over him and around him and through him.

Like he was too small to matter.

Nobody turned. Nobody saw him. His voice vanished into all the rest.

A grown man slammed into him and did not even look back.

A woman smashed into him with enough force to make his ribs hurt. Lantern glass broke somewhere underfoot. Something wet splashed his ankle. He looked down and saw red on the stones and thought paint, stupidly, stupidly because festival things spilled all the time and because his head would not let it be anything else.

Then someone stepped in it and their boot came away red too.

Not paint.

Jory wiped at his face with his free hand and only made the tears worse.

He wanted his mother.

Needed to hear her voice.

Needed Marla crying nearby. Crying meant she was alive.

Instead, there were too many voices and none of them were for him.

A group of grown-ups shoved down a narrower lane to his left. They looked like they knew where to go. That had to mean safe. Didn't it?

So, Jory followed them.

Not because he thought it was right.

Standing still meant getting trampled.

The road smelled strange almost at once.

It smelled sharp and bitter, like when lantern oil spilled and somebody lit it by mistake. But it was bigger. Thick enough to sting his nose. Thick enough to make his throat feel too small to breathe.

Smoke, he thought.

Cooking smoke, maybe.

The people ahead of him were coughing now, one hand over their mouths, the other dragging children or holding skirts or pushing through with their shoulders lowered. Someone shouted that there was room ahead. Someone else shouted that there wasn't. A man with blood down one side of his face said, "Go, go, go!"

Jory went.

Everyone else was going.

There was no place left for him to stay.

If he wanted to find his mother, he could not stay still.

Then he saw shapes through the smoke.

At first, he thought of the performers. Festival men. Painted men. Men in masks, maybe.

He was wrong.

Tall shapes in dark coats, moving the way men moved when they knew everybody was looking at them. His mind thought festival before it could understand fear.

Then one of them lifted an arm.

Light broke from it.

It cracked through the lane with a sound like the sky splitting open, and the people in front of Jory flew sideways all at once.

The air filled with a burned, sour smell he did not know.

One man hit the wall hard enough to make a sound Jory would hear in his sleep for the rest of his life.

Another folded where he stood and did not get back up.

Someone screamed for Heir to save them.

Another screamed for Grace to protect them.

Jory dropped with the rest of the grown-ups.

The stones smashed his knees.

His hands were scraped raw.

Something heavy hit the back of his head, and bright white sparks burst behind his eyes.

For one stupid second he thought the fireworks had followed him down.

All he heard was loud ringing.

Boots came through the smoke, but Jory couldn't focus enough to lift his head.

They were heavy boots.

Tall shapes walked past like the things his cousins swore lived outside the walls after dark.

He curled in on himself so hard it hurt, pressing his face into his arm and trying not to breathe at all. If he stayed small enough, maybe they would not see him.

No one looked down.

For once, that felt like the only good thing left in the world.

One pair of boots stopped so close he felt the air move when they hit the ground.

They moved on.

When he finally lifted his head, the road looked nothing like the bustling streets of festivities.

A man lay on the stones with one eye open so wide he no longer looked human.

A woman was trying to push herself up with an arm that bent wrong in the middle, blackened ash covering her dress.

Someone else was on fire for only a second before two other people beat it out with their hands.

A child's doll lay face down in something dark and wet.

Jory stared at the open eye.

Not the rest of the man.

Just the eye.

The image burned permanently into his mind.

A voice nearby kept saying, "No, no, no, no," in the same voice over and over.

His heart was beating so hard he could feel it in his throat.

He swallowed, and nothing went down.

This was not from the festival.

Not a fight. Not shouting. Not something grown-ups could make normal.

This was real.

His mother was not here.

Marla was not here.

Another crash shook the path as the chimney to a nearby building came tumbling down and crushed the people beneath it.

The roar broke whatever frozen piece of him had been left.

He stopped being able to stay there.

He ran.

Back out of the path. Past the bent arm. Past the smell of burning and ash and stone and whatever it was that clung to the smoke and made him want to be sick.

He burst into a wider road where the panic had somehow grown worse. A cart had overturned. One wheel still spun uselessly. A horse screamed and kicked against its harness. Someone was trying to lift a beam pinning another man beneath it. A woman stumbled by with half her sleeve burned away and a child in her arms that never moved once.

Jory spun in place, turning too fast, trying to find anything that looked familiar.

His mother's coat.

Her hair.

Marla's mud stained shoes.

Anything.

Nothing.

Everything was smoke and people and noise and too much air above him.

The buildings felt taller than they should have been. His eyes could not stay still.

He could not get enough air, no matter how hard he tried.

Everything around him had gotten too big all at once.

Then he caught the sight of a little girl sitting in the middle of the road and screaming for her father.

She was smaller than Marla. Not Marla. Relief came first, quick and mean, and then something worse right behind it.

A man was moving against the crowd instead of with it, shoving broken boards aside and lifting people up when they fell. Jory only saw him clearly for a moment.

When everything had become boots and elbows and smoke and screaming.

The man looked right at him. Not past him like everyone else. At him.

The little girl in the road vanished beneath a wave of bodies.

"Hey—" Nothing came out.

His chest was fluttering too fast. Too tight. He could not pull a full breath in.

He could only stare at the place where the little girl had been and know that if he had been smaller, if he had gone down harder, that would have been him.

The man dragged someone back to his feet, then turned toward Jory and barked something sharp enough that Jory obeyed before he even understood it.

Move, maybe.

Run?

Get up?

It didn't matter.

Jory moved.

Because the man's hand clamped onto his shoulder and yanked him hard against his side just as another wave of bodies came tumbling through.

Jory hit the man hard enough to lose his footing. The man staggered, caught himself, and turned his own body into a wall between Jory and the crush for one breath, then another.

Boots slammed past. Someone crashed into the man's back hard enough to jerk them both sideways. Jory heard wood crack somewhere close and thought the wagons were coming down around him.

Then he shoved Jory toward the narrow gap between the wagons. "Go!"

Jory stumbled through the gap, his eyes half-blind with tears and smoke.

Behind him he heard the stampede hit where he had just been.

His mother was gone. So was Marla.

He didn't know if that little girl had made it through or been crushed where she sat.

Or if the man who shoved him toward safety was still standing or already dead.

All he knew was that Fall Lake was screaming, and he was still inside it.

CHAPTER 3: THE WEIGHT OF DUTY

RIVIN

He spent the better part of the ride back to Fall Lake telling himself Saria would still be angry when he got home.

He preferred that version.

Anger meant she had waited up. That she was standing in the doorway with one hand on her hip and the other steadying Ronan where the boy leaned against her leg, half asleep from too much sugar and too much excitement.

He adjusted the strap of his spear across his back and rolled one sore shoulder beneath his cloak. The ride back from training had left every man in the detachment stiff and dust-covered. Kingsguard did not complain when officers could hear it. They straightened. They answered. They endured.

Rivin had always been good at that.

His father had been good at it. His grandfather before him. Saintcloud men had stood in armor longer than Rivin had been alive, and he had been raised to believe there was honor in being the one who held a line while others slept safely behind it. There had been pride in that lesson. There still was, most days.

Tonight felt different.

"You planning to ride through your own front door in that face?" one of the guards beside him asked.

Rivin glanced over. Bailen. Broad jaw, crooked nose, old scar splitting one eyebrow. The kind of man who found a joke in anything so long as it was aimed somewhere else first.

"My face is fine."

Bailen barked a laugh. "Your wife won't think so. She might finally leave you for a better looking man."

"Keep dreaming."

The men ahead of them chuckled quietly. Rivin ignored them. He reached into the pouch at his belt and thumbed over the small wooden carving inside. It was no craftsman's work. Quiet hours on post had given him time to cut it himself, shaving away at a scrap of wood until something horse-shaped remained. One ear was uneven. One leg was thicker than the others.

Ronan would love it anyway.

The boy had reached that age where anything his father handed him became a treasure at least for a day. Rivin had seen him carry around a smooth stone for three afternoons because he had been told it looked strong. He had named it Captain.

Fall Lake waited ahead, its outer rise catching the last color of evening. Even from a distance the city was dressed for Lunamani. Lantern lights glimmered. Roof edges shone with festival lights. From farther down, nearer the main roads, sound carried in bursts that the wind could not quite hold steady, full of music, laughter, shouting, and life.

Rivin fixed his eyes on it and sat a little straighter in the saddle.

He had missed the start of it. Missed the market hours. Missed whatever nonsense Ronan had surely talked Saria into buying him. He was tired of duty always arriving first and apology arriving after.

Still, he rode home in uniform.

His horse shifted beneath him. One of the officers up ahead raised a hand for the column to keep pace and Rivin obeyed without thinking, eyes still fixed on the city.

That was when the first tremble rolled over the hills and rippled the lake water.

It wasn't music. It wasn't thunder either.

Deep and broad. The sound resonated in his ribs before it caught his ears.

The horses reacted first. Tossing their heads and shifting in their place as their riders yanked them back in line.

Rivin's hand went to the reins out of instinct. He turned in the saddle and looked toward the city again.

"What was that?" Bailen asked quietly.

None answered. They only tried to see ahead.

Another sound followed, louder this time, deep enough to send the lake water splashing against the shore. Followed by screams, scattered at first, then gathering into something more central.

The officer at the front raised his fist, calling for a halt as several began to bring their horses forward.

The detachment slowed in a ripple of iron, leather, and snorting breath. Riders turned. Men shaded their eyes and peered toward Fall Lake. Someone behind Rivin prayed to Heir under his breath.

A shape climbed above the roofline in the distance, dull and gray.

Rivin felt his chest tighten at once as he watched the smoke rise.

"Hold," the officer barked again. "Hold formation."

The detachment steadied.

A rider came hard from the direction of the city. He nearly lost control as he slowed just enough. "Breach in the city. Fires spreading."

"By what?" their lead officer asked.

The rider looked like he did not know whether to answer or be sick. "Something big. Magic in the streets. The crowd broke. Orders are to secure the northwestern road and keep it open for evacuation."

Rivin never looked at the man. His eyes stayed on the smoke.

His home sat on the northern section. Saria would have taken the market paths back if the crowds turned ugly. Unless she had stayed longer, Ronan begging for one more stop or sightseeing. Or possibly they had gone to watch the lake lights.

"Move," the officer snapped.

The detachment moved without question. Training took hold. Horses turned as boots pressed stirrups. Soldiers shifted from weary return to immediate readiness.

Rivin obeyed the command.

By the time they reached the lower road, the first civilians were already coming.

A woman without shoes. A man carrying a woman so limp in his arms that Rivin had to steel himself not to look away. Two older boys dragging someone between them whose legs no longer seemed willing to work. Festival ribbons were still tied to their wrists. Blood on sleeves. Ash in hair. Faces gone pale with shock.

"Keep moving," the officer shouted. "Stay to the sides. Keep the center clear. Get them out."

Kingsguard dismounted and moved into practiced order. Some took the horses back. Others formed lanes. Rivin was sent with four men to keep wagons from clogging the crossing where the road narrowed against an old retaining wall. It was sensible and necessary.

"Sir," he said, stepping to the officer as another flood of screaming civilians spilled around the bend, "my family is in the upper district."

The officer did not even look at him. He was pointing, directing, counting numbers, making sense where there was none.

"Then pray they ran sooner than the others."

"Permission to go find them."

That caught a glance from his officer.

"No."

Rivin stood still for half a breath too long.

"Your post is here, Saintcloud."

Another cart came lurching down the slope, one wheel broken, three people hanging off either side of it. A pony screamed when it hit the ditch.

Rivin swallowed whatever response had risen in him and turned to help right the cart and its passengers.

For a while there was no room left in him for anything but motion. Lift. Pull. Catch the child before they fell. Move the wounded left. Keep the road clear. Answer the same terrified questions with the same meaningless words.

This way. Keep moving. Stay together. You are clear once you pass the bend. Follow the road to Riversend.

His hands knew their work. His body knew where to stand and how to make people listen when panic made them deaf. He hauled a beam off a crushed wagon. He put a sobbing old man back on his feet. He steadied a mother so she would not lose her grip on her daughter. He shouted until his throat burned. He called out over roars and fire and bursts and collapsing buildings that fell apart too fast compared to how long it took to build.

All the while, Fall Lake kept burning above them.

The smoke rolled higher. More screams broke over the walls and across the water in frightened waves.

Over the rooftops, Rivin saw a flash of light so violent and blue it carved the whole skyline sharp for a heartbeat. The men around him froze. One crossed himself with the old sign of the Gracemother.

Rivin knew exactly where it came from. What district it was in. He didn't know the source, not yet. Too many words spoken over one another as men, women, and children escaped the city.

Saria was likely calming Ronan. He would listen, being brave because his mother told him to.

Another rush of civilians hit the road. This time he caught a glimpse of the baker that lived just a few buildings from him.

Rivin caught him by the shoulder. "The upper rise. Saria. Ronan. What happened?"

The man's eyes were wide and wet. "Fire," he got out. "I, I don't know. It went through everything."

Rivin let go and the man was gone without hesitation.

He found his officer again twenty minutes later, maybe five, could have been an hour. Time had stopped keeping shape. The road had become nothing but bodies in motion and orders spoken louder than fear.

"Sir."

The officer turned with irritation already on his face, then seemed to remember who stood in front of him. Ash had settled into the lines at the corners of his eyes. One side of his jaw was smeared with dark ash. He looked older than he had an hour before, and likely they all did.

Rivin kept his voice level. "The north line is holding. Bailen and Coris can keep the wagons moving. Let me go."

"No."

"My home is on the upper rise."

"I know where your home is, Saintcloud."

The answer hit harder than it should have. The officer was not being cruel. He understood exactly what Rivin was asking and denied him anyway.

Rivin steadied his breath, drawing it slowly in through his nose and letting it out again. His father used to say a man who could not hold his own breath could not hold a shield wall either.

"With respect, sir, if they're still inside, I can't waste time."

"And if this road clogs, every moment will matter here as well. You aren't the only one with family in the city, kid."

Rivin's eyes were already past him, toward the broken stream of people still pouring down from Fall Lake. A man with half a sleeve burned away stumbled through the ditch and nearly dragged three others down with him. Two guards caught him before he fell. A wagon was coming too fast and nearly ran over several others.

The officer stepped closer and lowered his voice. "I need soldiers, Saintcloud. Not husbands."

He clenched his jaw so hard he thought his teeth would crack. He said nothing because anything he gave voice to in that moment would be the wrong thing.

The officer mistook silence for obedience. "Back to your post."

It took everything in him to nod and turn. Men were watching. They knew his name, and Saintcloud men did not make scenes in front of a line that needed holding. He took three steps before he heard another crash from the city and stopped just long enough to look uphill.

Smoke continued to roll over the city walls, the top of the watchtower now devoured by it. It was his duty to return to work.

A man was pinned under the hull of a wagon. Rivin and Bailen lifted it enough for two others to drag him free. The man screamed when they pulled him loose, and Rivin saw then that the wagon had not pinned the leg so much as finished what something else had started. Rivin told two of the younger guards to get him to the designated side for the wounded and keep the path clear. He repeated it twice when one of the boys froze at the blood.

"Move him, now!"

A young mother came through next with two children and no shoes, her dress half burned away exposing more of her leg than she intended. Scorched flesh showed beneath the torn hem. She should have been on the ground from the pain alone, but she kept moving. She couldn't stop with the children still in her hands. She kept looking back as she hurried, scanning the road behind her as though someone might still come barreling through the smoke after them.

"Careful, madam. Keep moving." Rivin guided her toward the road.

"My husband was behind us. He stopped and told us to keep going."

"He will follow soon. Keep on the road."

"He, he, he. Told us to run and not stop."

Rivin put a hand on her shoulder, guiding her toward the road. He kept his grip gentle, the woman was already trembling hard enough to shake her children too. "Then honor that, get your children to safety."

She stared at him for one broken heartbeat, then nodded and stumbled forward.

A panicked horse pushed through the path, its rider dangling from the side lifelessly. Bailen and Rivin took hold of it before it trampled a line of wounded near the retaining wall.

Rivin pressed the heel of one hand against his sternum, as if that could somehow ease the pressure gathering there. He was breathing too shallow. He knew it. He also knew better than to feed it. Panic would grow uncontrollable if given the room.

He counted the current situation instead. Wagons through, six. Mounted wounded sent down the road, three. Children unaccompanied, four.

He focused on the numbers. Easier to manage than everything else.

An officer further toward the city shouted. "The west road is clear enough. Rotate the front line in."

Rivin was already in motion before the words had settled.

His officer was already barking fresh assignments. Half the men at the road would remain. The rest were to move in by squad and start pushing survivors toward the lower shelters, clearing routes where they could, putting out fires where they could not. This was not the permission he wanted, but it was both worse and better than that. It was duty again, only now pointed toward the city. Closer to Saria and Ronan.

He did not wait to hear his name. He was already moving to retrieve his spear when the officer caught his eye.

"Saintcloud. With me."

The relief hit Rivin like pain. One step closer.

They advanced at a hard pace up the northwestern approach, five guards wide at first and then breaking narrower as the streets tightened. The smoke made every breath scratch. Rivin drew part of his cloak across his mouth and kept scanning ahead, every instinct sharpened now that he was finally moving toward the place his thoughts had never left.

The first body he recognized was a cooper from a few streets over. Rivin knew him only by sight and by the way he used to sing badly when carrying barrels from cart to cellar. The man lay half across a pile of broken crates with his head turned too far to one side. Rivin's eyes caught on him for only a moment, then the broken wall that had likely crushed him. He moved on.

The second body was harder to look at. A seamstress Saria used whenever they could spare the coin. One shoe missing. One wrist bent the wrong way.

The city was louder inside than it had been from the road, but it was a different kind of loud. Not a great cry. Pieces of it merging and separating into fragments, each line adding weight to his steps. A man shouting for his partner. Men straining together under fallen stone. The crack and spit of fire feeding on beams and cloth. Somewhere farther in, a horse screamed the way animals did when pain reduced them to instinct.

This quarter looked as though someone had tried to stomp the heart out of it. Stalls were overturned. Tables split. Lantern lines had snapped and dragged across the stones. He stepped over spilled fruit ground slick into the stones and a child's ribbon darkened by ash. A sweetbread lay crushed flat near a doorway, a child's hand stretched toward it, lifeless.

He saw Ronan everywhere in the wreckage without actually seeing him once. A little wooden whistle in a gutter. Tiny footsteps stamped into the ashen road. Every small thing became him for a blink and then became someone else's grief instead.

"Saintcloud." The officer's voice snapped him back. "Left lane. Check for movement."

Rivin peeled off without answer and took two others with him into a narrower run of homes and small shops just above the quarter's north edge. The lane should have felt familiar. He had walked it in winter snow and summer heat, with Saria's arm through his own after dinner.

A roof beam had collapsed across the path ahead. Smoke bled through the gaps. He and the other men wedged their spears and used both hands to free the wood. He lifted with the guards beside him until they could shift enough debris for the third man to crawl through and check the other side.

The man shook his head solemnly. "No one alive."

They let the beam drop and moved on. Their house stood farther uphill just off the bend where the baker's lane opened into the rise. Rivin knew the exact number of paces between the corner post and his front step. He also knew, before he reached it, that the door was hanging wide open.

He broke into a run.

The yard fence had been crushed inward. Their front shutter torn loose and dangling from one hinge. He hit the doorway hard enough to slam it against the wall.

"Saria!" he shouted.

No response.

He crossed the room in three strides, spear forgotten, the guard behind him saying something he did not catch. He scanned the room too quickly to spot anything in detail, but that was not what he was searching for. Ronan's blanket lay under the bench. A clay bowl had been shattered. But the thing he looked for most wasn't there.

No bodies. No blood. They weren't here.

Hope rushed back so fast it nearly toppled him to his knees.

He turned and searched properly this time.

The bedroom, empty.

The storage room, empty.

Ronan's room, empty.

His chest ached. Hope had risen fast, and despair rose with it.

Outside he went.

Where would Saria have gone?

Not the docks. Too crowded. Not the high square. Too exposed. She would choose shelter first once the panic turned real. Walls. Passages. Somewhere Saria could keep Ronan close and out of the worst of the panic. He caught sight of a shape in the distance and ignored it. His mind was too focused to care.

Saria knew the city almost as well as he did. Likely better. She would think ahead to the foolish things men forgot.

From his pouch, he pulled the carved figure that would have been found scattered across this floor and held it against his chest.

A voice from the street shouted his name. One of the guards from his squad.

"Any sign?"

His silence said everything.

The man pointed downhill. "We're pushing survivors toward the Lake Gate passage. Heard some families were sent there earlier."

Earlier. Not dead then. She would keep moving. She wouldn't stop. She was the smartest person he knew.

His feet moved faster than he could even think. The soldier hadn't even finished talking when Rivin pushed so hard past him the man had to catch himself to keep from falling.

He cut through the back alley to avoid the heaviest crowd. Boots slipped on grime, mud, blood, and Heir only knew what else.

The Lake Gate shelter sat in a section of Fall Lake where the walls had been thickened against floodwater. It had been built to last. It was not enough.

People lay outside the entrance. Some still. Others moved weakly. One man crawled there, barely able to drag himself against the wall.

Rivin's feet slowed but his eyes didn't.

He stepped over a broken lantern frame, then over a body yet to be cleared of the streets. A body was being pulled from an archway, but he didn't stop.

Heat still clung to the stone here. The entrance had burned. Smoke and embers sat thick in the air, and every sound near the shelter came thin and strained.

The faces blurred together near the entrance. An old man. A young girl with half her face and hair burned away.

He moved deeper, ears pulsing with a thudding heat that crossed his vision.

Collapsed wood and stone caught his attention near the inner wall. A strip of blue cloth pinned beneath it.

His heart stopped before his feet did. But the room did not go as quiet as he did. Men were still shouting outside. Someone nearby was praying. The sounds of screams and cries and the ruin of Fall Lake still stirred farther away.

His grip tightened on the little carving until the wood bit into his palm.

The world had not gone silent. Men still shouted. Someone still prayed. The city still burned within the walls. But all of it had stepped away from him. Blue was the only color left.

Not just any blue. The blue of the lake under clear weather. The blue he liked best on her.

Rivin took one step forward.

Then another.

Then he saw the curve of an arm. Then a wrist. The glint of silver on a hand, curled around a smaller one.

He stood breathless, his throat filled with lead. His fingers uncurled, and the wooden horse soundlessly dropped into the blood and ash at his feet.

CHAPTER 4: THE HANDS OF GRACE

AVANNA

"Hold him… Hold!"

The table jolted as the man thrashed, blood slicking the wood beneath him. Avanna shoved her forearm across his chest, forcing him down as another sister drove a needle through torn flesh that refused to stay closed.

"He's bleeding through it again."

"I see it!"

The stitch tore the moment it tightened.

Blood followed.

"Gods, where is—"

The man screamed. Not words. A shriek that cut through the room.

Avanna leaned harder. Ribs shifted beneath her weight.

"Still," she snapped, though he couldn't hear her over his own voice. "Don't you dare mo—"

A hand slammed a vial into her palm.

"Azure!"

She didn't look, just uncorked it with her teeth and poured.

The liquid shimmered as it hit the wound, blue bleeding into red. Forcing it back into place. The flesh tightened. Knitted together. Fought. Then it split again.

"Gods—"

The blue shimmer fought like it always did. Azure didn't heal so much as remind the body what to do, and this was too much.

"He's losing too much!"

Another scream cut through the room. Then another. Then more. Now they all blurred together.

Avanna shoved the empty vial aside.

"More!"

"That was the last one."

"Find more!"

"They're already—"

"Get it!"

The sister ran.

Or tried to.

She tripped over a body laid out on the floor, someone too far gone for a table, and hit the ground hard enough to lose her breath.

No one helped her up. Every hand was already taken.

The man's movements slowed. He was fading.

"No. Not yet," she said under her breath.

She shifted, fingers in the wound. The puncture was massive, ripped open by Zenith knew what. Beam. Claw. Tooth. It did not matter.

Her fingers slipped inside it. There was no clean edge. Something inside had been torn loose, but she couldn't find it.

The man's scream broke into a wet choke. Blood filled his mouth, spilling over the prayer table.

Avanna turned his head so he wouldn't drown in it.

Screams. Voices. Men, women, children. All at once.

Fingers wrapped around her arm. Her dress pulled from another hand.

"Please."

She shook them off without looking.

"Stay with me," she said quietly.

This stitch held.

For a moment. Then it burst open again.

"Avanna!"

She didn't look.

"Avanna, I need you, now!"

"Not now, Idra!"

"He's—"

"I said not now!"

"There's nothing below his ribs!"

Her eyes snapped to it before she could stop herself. She shouldn't have looked.

Across the room, a man lay on another makeshift table, or what was left of him. Everything below his ribs was gone. Torn and crushed, not clean but torn apart by something impossible.

Blood pulsed. Everything below his ribs was ruin.

One of the younger sisters stood over him, frozen, hands covered in blood that had nowhere to go. He was awake, alive, somehow.

"I don't know what to do," she said, voice shaking. "I don't, there's nothing to—"

"There is always something."

But she didn't move.

"Gracemother be with us."

The man beneath her table coughed.

Weak and wet. Barely alive.

The woman at her feet lifted an infant toward Avanna, still as could be. Pleading and begging.

"She's just cold," she said. "She's just cold."

She kept saying it. Repeatedly like the words would change.

"Finish him!" Someone shouted.

"He's gone, leave him, help me."

"Please save her."

"Heir has him now."

"Please, please, she's not waking up."

"My brother, he can't feel his legs."

"She was burned."

"Teeth."

"They were throwing fire."

"Collapsed."

"It tore the street apart."

"It was taller than the walls, taller than—"

"That thing is still out there."

"I was right next to her."

"Why are they on the tables and not us?"

"Because they got there first."

"She chose them over us."

Chose. The word engraved itself into her mind.

She pushed it down.

No time.

"Azure."

"There's barely any left!"

"Then stop wasting it!"

Avanna moved. Sweat, blood, and Azure slick across her skin. She continued to stitch the man, pressed and bandaged another with her other arm, directed a younger sister on setting a shoulder back in place.

Halsric moved through the chaos like a boulder down a steep incline, grabbing a man by the shoulders as he tried to force his way forward. He never hesitated over who to move or where to stand. The widest part of him always found the doorway first.

"Stand down," Halsric said.

"My wife is dying!"

"So is everyone else!"

"I don't care about everyone else, save h—"

"Move or I move you."

He shoved them off. Cleared the doorway. Planted in place.

Bodies had already been moved too many times.

Avanna's patient spasmed again.

Then went slack.

No.

She pressed against his chest. Nothing. Harder. Nothing.

"Come on," she said. "Come on!"

A sister came beside her, a hand placed on her back.

"He's—"

"No!"

Avanna pressed again, as white tendrils of mana formed from her hands, pushing on his sternum. It burned inside him.

There. A flicker.

"He's not done."

Barely a breath. Slipped away as fast as it came.

She pressed again.

Nothing.

The skin cooled beneath her hands.

Gone.

Across the room, a man let out a gurgling choke.

The young sister backed away from him. "I can't—"

Avanna shouted from across the room, "You can. Again."

"I can't fix that."

"Then keep him alive."

"That's not—"

"Do your job."

She was spent. Mana drained from too much healing.

The young girl had frozen in place.

Then moved again, hands trembling. She tried anyway, forcing a healer's reed between his ribs. The first push missed.

"Again."

The second went in. Blood spilled out.

Avanna didn't remember finishing.

Or remember moving.

She was already at the next.

The walls closed in on her.

Too loud.

Voices pressed in over each other.

Until they weren't voices anymore. Only pressure.

Blood filled her eyes. Not hers.

Her hands were shaking. They wouldn't stop.

"Please, just look at him."

"Help me, please."

"She's choosing who lives."

One of the voices cut off. No one knew which one it was.

"How do you get to decide?"

The words tightened around her heart and her head.

Tighter until every heartbeat seemed split from her skull.

A man shoved into her, grabbing her by the dress and shouting. "You're letting them die!"

Spit hit her cheek.

"You could save them if you tried!"

Avanna stood there. Hands still working.

She only stared and let Grace take her hands.

"Avanna."

Halsric. Close. But she didn't respond.

"Avanna."

Her jaw tightened. She pulled her hands away. Slowly and deliberately.

Halsric pulled the man off of Avanna and moved him to the side. He shouted something, but the words meant nothing.

"He's gone."

No one called his name.

Another body waited. Still alive.

Avanna stood, eyes glossed over, hands numbed but still moving. Her legs dragged. Every step felt too heavy, too slow. She was still too late.

Toward the shouting first.

Still fighting. Still loud.

Then, the quiet one. Not moving. Barely breathing.

She turned. She reached the man, looked down.

There was no fixing this.

No stitching. Not a potion.

No prayer or magic that could make this one whole again.

The young sister looked at her.

Waiting, hoping, and terrified. "Tell me what to do," she said, too calm now.

Everything closed in.

No time.

Her hand found his chest. What little breath was left.

She shook her head.

"Not this one. Make him comfortable. Stay with him."

The girl's face broke, eyes wide.

"No, please, there has to be—"

"There isn't."

"You don't know th—"

"I do."

The man made another sound. Weaker. Then nothing.

Avanna stepped back. Turned away and was already moving.

Behind her, the sounds stopped.

The door slammed shut behind her.

Silence, or near enough to it.

Avanna braced both hands against the wall. Her breath caught.

The hairs on her entire body stood on end. The tears came anyway. She pressed her forehead into the stone.

Trembling hands pressed into the wall until the tremors stopped.

They didn't stop. She just stopped noticing.

"I can't," she whispered, "I can't keep doing this."

Her voice broke.

She tried to swallow. Couldn't. The dread stuck in the back of her throat.

"Grace," she said, barely getting it out, "if you are here, if you hear me. Help me, I can't do this on my own. Goddess of Creation, Mother to Lyorion—"

"Avanna!"

"—I ask of you, give me the strength. Help me save at least some of them."

A hand struck the door.

"Avanna."

Tears wiped away, replaced by blood.

She steadied her breath.

"Coming."

Her voice didn't shake. She opened the door.

Noise poured back in like a wave. She stepped back into it anyway.

Halsric stood there.

Blood to the elbows and breathing heavy.

"We're losing them," he said.

"Not all of them."

No panic. No fear. Just the truth.

"We will not lose them all."

CHAPTER 5: THE WITNESS

EDWIN

A sleeve tore in his hands.

The thread snapped with it, biting into his finger as the man wearing it lurched forward, dragged uphill by someone else. Edwin caught the fabric on instinct, pressing his thumb along the split, easing the edges together as if it might still go back where it belonged.

It didn't.

The seam gave the rest of the way, opening beneath his fingers. The man twisted again, and then he was gone, pulled into the press of bodies moving toward the upper streets.

Edwin's hand lingered where it had been, fingers still pinched as if the cloth remained between them.

The seam had already given. Nothing left for it to catch.

People rushed past him in uneven waves.

Too fast, and too close.

He stepped back, brushing ash from his sleeve before it could settle. It smeared instead, darkening the fabric in a way he couldn't fix.

He had spent too much of the night watching things give way.

A woman stumbled near him, her dress torn open at the side. Edwin reached for her without thinking, fingers catching the edge of the rip.

"Just—"

She tore free and ran.

The fabric slipped from his grasp. The red cloth disappeared into the crowd, the color lingering in his mind longer than it should have. It deepened there, darkening into something that wasn't cloth at all before he blinked and it was gone.

He reached for someone else before he even knew who it was. A man clutching his side, coat hanging open where a seam had split from shoulder to waist. Edwin caught the edge of it, folding the cloth as he walked, fingers moving quickly, trying to keep it from dragging.

"Keep it closed," he said, pressing the fabric together with the flat of his hand. "Just hold it there."

The man nodded without understanding and kept moving.

Edwin's hand lingered, and he let go.

Someone collided with him from behind. He turned, catching a young woman by the shoulders before she fell. Her cloak had twisted around her neck, choking her movement.

"Wait!"

He untangled it quickly, pulling the clasp free, straightening it so it sat properly across her shoulders.

"There. Now go."

She didn't thank him. She didn't even look at him.

Edwin watched her briefly, then moved, searching for the next thing that could be set right.

Another fabric caught his eye near the edge of the street, pinned beneath a broken crate. Blue, finely woven, not work cloth. Something made for a better day.

He pulled it free.

It had torn clean along one side. Good fabric. Strong thread. It could have been mended properly with time.

He folded the edges without thinking, pressing it flat against itself.

A voice cut through the noise nearby.

"Have you seen her? She was right here, she was—"

Edwin looked up. A man turned in place, searching faces that would not stop moving long enough to be seen.

Edwin opened his mouth, then closed it.

He still held the cloth. For a moment he almost offered it, as if it might help.

Instead, he tucked it into his belt and turned away.

There were still things in front of him that needed hands.

The ground shifted beneath him.

Not from a collapse. Not the quick drop of failing structure.

Something moved through it.

It lifted him just enough that his weight came off his heels and settled wrong again. He felt it in his feet first, then in his hands, then in his teeth.

Edwin looked up without thinking.

Smoke dragged itself between buildings instead of rising clean. Through it, the lower streets broke in pieces that refused to fit together.

A wall folded inward.

Wooden beams snapped like they had been left to rot.

Something passed through it, not around it or over it, but straight through, as if the streets had no right to stand in its way.

It was too large to measure against anything he knew, and gone before he could understand.

He never saw it whole. Only pieces that refused to belong to one shape.

Magic split the air where nothing should have been. Tearing through the streets with force.

The front of a building collapsed as though struck from within.

"That isn't going to hold." Bodies would be crushed beneath it.

"Help him!"

The shout snapped him back.

A man was pinned beneath a fallen beam where a shopfront had given way in the road. It sat awkwardly, and Edwin saw it immediately. One end caught in stone, the other twisted into broken wood, all of it pressing inward instead of down.

He dropped beside them.

"Wait," he said, already reaching for the beam. "Not like that."

Two others were bracing to lift.

"We don't have time for that."

"If you pull it straight it'll—"

His words meant nothing once they felt the structure shift.

He ran his hand along the beam, following the fracture. The grain had split near a knot, failing along the weakest line, just like bad stitching always did. The stone beneath had shifted. If they lifted from the wrong point, the rest would drag forward.

Everything would come down.

His hands moved faster now, searching for something to adjust. A better angle, a place to wedge, a way to make it hold.

There wasn't one.

The man beneath the beam gasped. Edwin's attention dropped to him, and before anything else, his fingers went to the man's sleeve. It had twisted up under the pressure and fall.

He pulled it straight. Smoothing it flat.

Then his hand found the wound at the man's side.

Too much blood.

Edwin swallowed and reached for the small roll at his hip. Thread. Waxed cord. Tools for seams, not flesh.

But…

He threaded it.

"I know thread," he said, though he wasn't sure why he needed to say it aloud. "If I can close it—"

The first stitch went in wrong. He felt it immediately. Flesh didn't behave like cloth. It resisted. It would not pull clean.

The man cried out.

"Sorry, just, stay still."

Edwin tried again.

And again.

The needle bent slightly between his fingers. Not enough to snap. But enough that he felt it give. The waxed thread dragged against itself as he pulled, catching where it shouldn't.

He adjusted his grip, pulling the thread tighter on the next pass, trying to anchor it where the flesh would not hold. The knot slipped before catching in something deeper.

Blood seeped around the thread, undoing the work as quickly as he made it. He knew, even then, that he was sewing nothing closed. Only giving his hands something to do.

He kept going.

It wasn't good work. It wasn't even work that should have been done by him. But the wound was open, and thread was something he understood, and that was enough to make him keep going, if they got him free, maybe it would be enough.

The ground shifted again.

Stronger this time. Much closer.

The beam groaned.

Edwin felt the change through his palms, the others did too.

The structure shifted with each tremor, weight pulling in new directions.

He understood all of that. The same way that fabric and clothing worked, how they would bend and break, holding seams together.

"If we lift that," he said quietly, "it won't hold."

The man beneath looked at him.

"Please."

Edwin's hands tightened around it.

He pushed.

The beam lifted just enough for him to be pulled free.

Then dropped.

Stone above them cracked. The dust fell and the structure began to settle into something worse.

"Back," Edwin said.

The others hesitated.

"Get back."

He pulled one of them away himself. The other followed a moment later as the weight shifted and locked.

He screamed once.

Then not again.

He stayed too long, hands still shaped for work that no longer had a place to land, then forced himself to move.

The climb toward the castle had become a single frightened current.

People helped each other because they didn't know how not to.

A man carried someone who could not walk.

A stranger took a child from another's arms and passed her forward.

Someone handed water back down the slope even while climbing upward.

A boy stumbled near him, too small to keep his footing. Edwin caught him under the arms before he went down, pulling him close enough to steady.

He patted the shirt smooth. "There. Stay with them."

A man nearby was trying to lift an older woman, his grip slipping with every step. Edwin stepped in without asking, adjusting the man's hold before taking some of the weight himself.

"Under her arms," he said. "Not there. You'll lose her if someone bumps into you."

Together they managed to get her further up the hill.

The woman sagged once they stopped, her weight dropping fully into their arms. Edwin adjusted his grip without thinking, shifting her so her shoulder sat correctly.

"That's better."

Her breathing came shallow and uneven.

The man holding her looked at Edwin, waiting.

For instructions, or something.

There was nothing left for his hands to tie or mend.

"What do we do?" the man asked.

Edwin looked at her.

Then at him.

Then back at his hands.

"They'll take care of her up there," he said, nodding toward a crowd that appeared to be administering aid to others.

It sounded like something someone else would say. Someone who actually knew what to do.

The man nodded, clung to the woman and to Edwin's words.

Edwin moved along, helping whoever else was in front of him.

Straightening clothes before lifting, pulling sleeves down over burns, bandaging wounds with cloth.

"It'll hold," he said, tying off a strip of fabric.

Near the upper rise, people gathered behind broken stone.

Some crouched, others prayed.

Many just stared back down into the city as if trying to understand what they were seeing. The fire, dust, and smoke clouded much of the view. But the creature's size was visible even through it all, even if its details weren't.

Edwin sank down among them.

His hands kept moving. Brushing ash, smoothing fabric, turning his spool of thread without stopping.

Adjusting anything that would stay still long enough to be adjusted, again, and again.

"Please," his eyes caught the sky, a glimpse of something within it. "Please let this end."

The air felt heavy.

Not with heat or wind, or the burnt ash that filled the air.

The sky changed again.

Color cut through the smoke where only fire had cut before.

Red.

Blue.

Not lightning, nor flame.

Something else.

The sky stretched in a way that made his eyes ache.

"That's not—"

A crack followed.

Not from above. From everywhere around them. And it went through him.

Something drew his attention. His eyes were already locked in on the view.

A tower.

A man moving toward it.

Edwin's chest ached, though he couldn't have said why.

A fool, maybe. Or someone who had decided something he couldn't yet understand.

No one should have been there.

Everyone else moved away from the creature's path.

The beast shifted again, turning toward the rise.

Toward them.

Toward the tower.

The people pressed back.

Further uphill, screaming and yelling.

Away.

All except for that man.

He was moving toward the tower.

Edwin Marr stood watching.

The man moved to the highest point.

What would not hold, what no one could survive.

"What are you doing?" Edwin whispered to himself.

Edwin's gaze stayed fixated on him longer than it should have.

Everyone else was moving.

Pulling away.

Climbing higher.

But that man, he moved with a purpose.

Not running, or stumbling.

Like he had something waiting for him. His chest tightened, though he couldn't say why.

The man reached the top.

And with him, the entire city went still.

The prayers around Edwin stopped mid-word.

The drifting ash seemed to be stuck in place.

The sound of the city was distant.

Everything waited to see what the man would do.

"Good luck," he whispered.

The man moved.

Forward.

Edwin leaned in slightly, squinting through smoke.

Trying to understand.

Trying to piece it together.

He jumped.

The world fractured into pieces.

For a moment, it came into view in a way his mind could not process. Something vast, layered in motion and death, its shape breaking apart as soon as he tried to see it whole. The roar followed like thunder.

A roar that would have been enough to level a city on its own.

Light tore across the sky, too bright to follow cleanly. Red and blue streaked through it, not like lightning, not like fire, but something drawn downward with intent. The shape of the man was still there in it, falling, or pulled, or both at once. Edwin thought he saw something in his hand where nothing had been before.

Metal. No, not metal. Lightning. Not from the sky, but into him. Or from him.

The sound came all at once.

Not a single crack.

But many, blasting and breaking over each other until they became something else entirely.

Impact.

The ground struck back. A shockwave burst through the town.

It drove through Edwin, through the stone behind him, through the hill itself.

His vision tore red, then blue, then white.

The force didn't pass through the city. It dug into it.

The air folded, then burst outward, carrying dust, heat, and something thin that cut across his skin. Edwin felt himself thrown back against the stone behind him, the breath driven out of him in a single gasp.

He wasn't sure he was still on the ground.

Edwin's hands were still.

He didn't notice at first.

But when he did, he couldn't make them move again.

He stared at the place where it struck.

At what remained.

At the shape of what had been there before, now a space carved open where the tower used to be.

Something in him changed.

Not hope. Not relief.

Just a break in the certainty that anything could be fixed.

He tried to speak, but nothing came. There were no words for it, or he couldn't make them anymore.

Something pressed against his ribs. He couldn't tell what it was. When he tried to move, his body didn't answer the way it should have.

He drew a breath that didn't feel like it went anywhere.

Around him, shapes moved through the settling dust. People shouting. Others not moving at all.

He couldn't tell which he was.

His eyes stays fixated on the scene in front of him, as if looking away would undo whatever had just happened.

His hands still hadn't moved.

CHAPTER 6: THE ASHES AT DAWN

GAVIN

With the dust settled, the smoke didn't clear. It only thinned. Enough to see through, not enough to forget it was there or where it came from.

Gavin stood where he'd stopped.

Or close to it.

Hard to tell now.

Everything looked the same. Broken wood. Blackened stone. Shapes that didn't move. Some hadn't moved since the night. Others had only been dragged in.

Someone was calling names again. They had been all night.

Different voices. Same names. Spoken incorrectly. Whispered. Shouted. Calling out to some they knew—and others they didn't.

He bent over, fingers finding the edge of a plank half buried. It didn't want to move. He pulled anyway. Slow. No rush in it. A long scrape as splinters dragged across the stone.

There was a hand under it.

He stopped.

Looked at it.

No movement.

He didn't reach for it right away. Just breathed once through his sleeve. Then started clearing the rest. Piece by piece. Took longer than it needed to.

The body twisted as it came free.

Refused to look at the face.

He grabbed the wrist. Lifted. Set it back down.

Someone nearby said, "Hey, easy. Careful with them."

Gavin nodded.

"Mm."

He found a bit of cloth, and draped it over the body. Didn't line it up straight. Didn't fix it. Just covered enough.

A cart creaked behind him.

"Bring them this way," a woman called.

He didn't answer, just slid his hands under the shoulders. Lifted.

It was heavier than it should've been. Or maybe he was slower and weaker than he should've been.

Hard to tell.

He carried the body over. Set it down beside the others.

The bodies didn't fit right. None of them.

"Square," someone said. "Yeah, we're taking them to the square."

Gavin nodded.

"Mm."

The man waited like there might be more.

There wasn't.

Gavin went back.

Same direction. Same pace.

The ground shifted under his boots in places where it hadn't before.

Soft where it should've been solid.

Sticky where it shouldn't have been anything.

He stepped over something he didn't look at.

He slowed and looked back. Didn't go back for it. Kept walking.

A beam leaned against what used to be a wall. Gavin put his hand on it. Rested it there. The wood was still warm on one side, cold on the other.

He held that long enough he felt the heat fade from his palm.

Then he moved again.

There was a boot sticking out from under a pile of stone.

He recognized the leather. He knew the markings, and who wore it.

But he didn't stop.

If he bent for it, he would have to know for certain.

He kept walking.

Someone else would get it.

Or they wouldn't.

Two men were arguing near what used to be a doorway.

"Can't keep going like this. We need to move faster."

"With what?"

"With what we've got left."

"That's not enough."

"It has to be. We don't have anything else."

Gavin passed between them. Close enough to hear. Not close enough to be a part of it.

"You," one of them said. "Help us clear this?"

Gavin stopped.

Looked at the stones.

Then at the man.

"Mm."

He stepped in. Took hold of one edge. Waiting too long before lifting.

The other man had already started. They adjusted until they found a rhythm that didn't match. It worked anyway.

The stone shifted. Slid and dropped with a dull crack.

Dust kicked up. There was nothing below it.

"Next one."

Gavin nodded.

"Mm."

Did the same thing again. But slower this time.

On the third, Gavin's hands slipped.

Almost dropping it, he tightened his grip, didn't say anything.

He moved on after that.

Didn't say anything when he left.

There were more bodies the farther he went.

Some covered, some not.

He didn't look at faces.

He looked at hands.

At clothes.

At hair.

Height.

Weight.

Shoes.

Always the shoes.

A child's voice somewhere.

"Ma?"

Not loud. Just calling.

He didn't turn toward it.

Just kept moving.

Red cloth caught his eye.

He stopped and bent down. Picked it up, turned it over once.

He let it hang, then dropped it.

Not that one.

"Hey."

He didn't look right away.

"Hey."

He turned slower than he meant to.

A woman stood a few steps back. Ash covering her face. One side of her hair burned short. Hands shaking just enough to see it.

"Who you lookin' for? You been circlin'."

Gavin blinked.

Looked past her, then turned back.

"Just…working."

She stared at him.

"…same as you."

He kept walking before she could say anything else.

The sound had changed.

Less screaming.

More talking.

Quieter, heavier, many filled with tears and subtle cries.

People spoke like the air would break if they got too loud.

"I only stepped away for a second."

"I told him to stay put."

"He was right there. Right there."

The voice broke as Gavin stepped around them and moved on.

Another set of voices.

"They came out of nowhere."

"I saw Elfar. I'm telling you, I found their arrows everywhere."

"Doesn't matter what you saw. They aren't coming back."

Gavin stepped through them.

He found a few more half buried.

Kneeling took longer than it should've.

He stayed there before doing anything. Hands on his thighs. Breathing through his nose. Smoke still around him.

Then he started clearing.

Same as before.

Piece by piece.

Not rushing.

Not pausing.

Just slow.

He looked at their faces.

Didn't react.

Then adjusted the bodies.

Covered the face. Adjusted the limbs. Carried the body.

Arms shook now. Just enough to feel the shift when he carried them.

Didn't change how he moved.

At the cart, a man stood there. Younger, or less worn than others.

"You can stack them closer," he said.

Gavin set the body down. Adjusted it anyway. Not closer, just where it landed. The man watched, didn't argue. Just shook his head and moved on.

Gavin moved past. His hand caught the edge of a fence. Stopped without meaning to.

Someone bumped him.

"Come on, move."

He blinked. Looked at his hand. Pulled it away.

"…yeah."

The voices started low and didn't carry at first. Just another set of voices in the noise.

"They saw them."

"Elfar."

"They brought it here."

"They did this."

The voices layered over one another.

Feeding.

Building toward something.

More voices fell into the crowd.

Gavin stood at the edge of it.

Didn't step in, or away.

A man pushed forward. Face streaked with ash. Covered in blood. Didn't look like he noticed or cared.

"They came into our home—"

His voice cracked.

"They tear it apart—"

Shouts answered in agreement.

"They hide behind their forest while we bury our dead?"

More voices now, louder than before.

"We don't sit here. We're not doing that."

"We rally in Cyril. Gather what's left, then we make them answer!"

Another voice cut through.

"We lost enough. We don't need more of this."

A woman this time.

Not yelling, but loud enough to carry over the noise.

The first man shook his head.

"We already lost everything. What do I have left to lose?"

Someone near Gavin said, "He's right."

Gavin's eyes moved over them. One by one.

A man stood near the front.

Bandage wrapped over one eye. Blood seeped through it. He wasn't speaking. Just standing. Watching.

The voices kept rising.

Fists clenched.

Hands shaking.

People needing somewhere to put their rage.

"You coming?"

Not meant for him.

The man stood next to him.

Expectant and waiting.

Gavin looked at him.

Held it a second too long.

Blinked.

"…Hard to tell."

The man looked at him like it wasn't enough. Like he should have been met with the same rage.

It didn't change anything. Gavin left them to it.

The sounds followed him for a while. Then faded.

He found it near a collapsed stall. He knew it before he picked it up.

He lifted it. Turned it in his hands, slower than before.

She had this.

He held onto that thought and tucked it beneath his fingers.

Looked over what was left.

Smoke still rising.

People still moving.

Names called over each other. He didn't know why that mattered. No one was answering back.

He went back to the cart. Hands found the edge and pulled.

The wheels rolled. Same sound. Same rhythm.

The path to the square was clearer now.

More people moving that way.

Carrying, dragging, walking. Some limping. Some not stopping.

No one spoke to him.

He didn't speak. Just listened.

"I should've gone back."

Another voice answered.

"You wouldn't have made it. You know that."

"I don't care, I should've gone anyway."

Gavin kept walking.

The sun pushed through the smoke.

Didn't quite break it.

Just made it easier to see.

And worse to look at.

The cart rolled.

Bodies shifted slightly with each bump.

Different names were called as they moved deeper in. No answers, no responses.

What was left of the square came into view.

People were already there.

Laying them down.

Row by row, single paths with enough room for people to walk through.

They pulled the cart to the side.

He stood there too long.

He started unloading.

One at a time.

Same as before.

Lift. Carry. Set down. Stand up. Go back.

Several of them were smaller. He paused before lifting. Finished his motions.

No names.

No words.

When the cart was empty, he didn't move right away.

He stood there, looking over the rows.

Too many to count. Too many burned. Too many smashed. Too many impaled. Too many in pieces.

Someone brushed past him, carrying another.

He turned and walked back the way he came.

Same path.

Smoke still filling lungs.

The sounds repeating.

Names ignored.

The smoke hadn't cleared. Just thinned.

He passed the boots again.

He still didn't stop.

The voices were quieter, or he was.

He kept moving. He kept getting more bodies.

Behind him, someone said they were leaving by midday. Gathering what they could in Cyril. Marching for Aevoridge.

His arms were trembling now.

Gavin didn't remember when the light changed.

Only that the moons were gone and the sun had risen.

He walked through the same street again. Or a different one. Hard to tell.

The landmarks didn't hold anymore. Walls were gone where they should've been. Doors opened into nothing. Streets bent where they used to run straight.

He slowed near half a doorway that still stood. A single chair was the only thing inside.

A man knelt in the street a few paces ahead.

Not moving.

Not working.

Just kneeling.

Gavin passed him. Looked back.

The man's hands were empty. Nothing in front of him but the ground. Like he'd forgotten what he was supposed to be doing.

Gavin watched him for a moment.

A body lay half in the road.

Not covered yet.

Gavin stopped.

Shoes first.

He bent. Lifted. Moved. Set and covered.

Someone stumbled past him carrying a bundle of something he couldn't tell.

They were whispering.

Not to him.

Not to anyone.

"I've got you."

Repeatedly.

"I've got you."

Gavin never turned.

The cart waited where he'd left it. Or where someone had put it back.

It didn't matter.

It was there. He took hold. Didn't pull. Just stood.

His arms fought back, too heavy to use.

He forced them to. Pulling. Dragging the wheel. Same sound. Louder than it should've been.

Another body.

Then another.

Then another.

He couldn't remember finding all of them. Lifting. Placing. Setting the cloth over them.

He kept moving and tried not to stop. He knew, if he did stop, nothing would change.

It didn't bring them back.

He bent. Got his hands under. Lifted. Walked. Set the weight down. Turned. Went back.

Bend. Lift. Move. Set. Pull. Wheel. Same sounds. Same boots.

There wasn't anything else to do.

Fall Lake had stood in celebration.

Now it grieved.

Someone still had to pull the cart.

WHAT CARRIED FORWARD

SPOONY

No one reached for their drink. No chair scraped. Even the fire settled low, like it had heard enough and was ready to call it a night.

The room didn't move.

That's how I knew they stayed with it.

I kept my hand on the table a moment longer, my spoon resting with it.

Then I drew a breath.

"Now… that's the part people don't tend to keep."

A few of them adjusted in place. Others leaned back, relieved it was over. One man still hadn't touched the drink in front of him all night. Still, he paid.

I glanced toward the bar.

He was already moving again, slow and steady behind the counter, like nothing in the world had changed except the number of empty cups. Red hair slipped between tables with a fresh round, smiling like she always did. Green barely made a sound at all, just there to refill or clean, then gone.

A muffled curse followed the clatter behind me.

I didn't have to look to know who it was in the kitchen.

"Careful," I'd told him before. *"He bites when he thinks you've earned it."*

The room laughed at the situation. Good. They needed that.

I tapped the table once with the spoon.

"Most folk remember the clean part of it. The part that makes legends or villains."

I gave a shrug, smirking.

"Hard not to. Lightning split the sky. Man on the tower. Hammer falling to his hand. Beast going down like the world had finally had enough."

A man near the back nodded. "That's the part worth remembering."

"Is it?" I said openly, just asking.

He didn't answer.

I let that sit for several seconds.

"They're not wrong, mind you," I went on. "That part happened the same as anything else."

I leaned against the table.

"But it's easier to tell it that way. Shorter, and kinder to the ones who came for a legend."

I rolled my thumb along the edge of the spoon without thinking.

"But it leaves out everything that makes the story worth hearing or gives it meaning."

A woman near the front spoke up, quietly. "Like what?"

"Like who thought they were about to die. And who never got to bury their own."

My eyes moved past her. She was settled with my answer, no matter how unpleasant.

"Consider the ones who had to make it through, witness to all of it—and still had to wake up after."

No one spoke to that.

"You don't hear that in bard's tales or a song. It doesn't carry well."

I wanted to kick my feet on the table, but the time wasn't right.

"Thing is… all of it happened at the same time."

I gestured loosely toward the door, at the world outside, though none of us could see it from here.

"Same night. Same streets. Same sky above it."

A thump behind me, I didn't need to glance back to know, the culprit darted past feet and up onto the back of a chair like he owned it.

"See?" I said with the world making my point. "Not everything lands where it's supposed to, and the world doesn't stop just because we need it to."

A few chuckles were enough to help ease the room.

"I didn't gather those stories because anyone asked for them."

A slight shake of my head.

"Most people don't. And they wouldn't."

My hand rested flat on the table, on the recovered stories of old. Many late nights. Adventures. Stories for another day that brought these back to us.

"People talk about hope like it shows up all at once."

I tapped the spoon on the table as another book lifted onto it. "Big moment. Bright lights. Something you can point to and say, there it is."

I tilted my head down a little. "Hasn't been my experience."

A couple of people moved at that. Quiet voices started at one table, then died just as quickly.

"And sometimes—it lands in someone who didn't go looking for it."

My grin answered, flipping my spoon into the air.

"You know who I mean. The one who brought the beast down." No name to be said. "The one who caught the hammer." Someone near the front let out a held breath. They'd heard it before, but not like that.

My spoon dropped clean back into my hand, and I struck the table with it. The book snapped open, pages tearing forward in bursts of white light.

The patrons leaned in, some smiling, some amazed at the display.

"People like to say he stood alone." I shook my head.

"He didn't. What reached him that night—"

The pages slowed.

"—wasn't just iron."

The fire popped and burst.

"And whatever started there—"

I let the sentence trail off.

"—didn't end when it hit the ground."

I pushed off the table, landing on my feet, startling the patrons enough to follow and rise.

"Stories like those don't end when the noise stops,"

I pointed the spoon at each of them.

"They don't wrap up neat just because the worst part's over."

The small companion ran circles around their feet.

"Some things don't stay where they happen." My voice dropped. "They carry farther than they were meant to. They linger on the ones still standing."

I tapped the spoon one last time against the table.

"If you want to know what came of it—then you follow the man."

I paused.

"Because the rest of it… didn't stay behind."

EXCERPT: IGNITING HOPE

Running blind, it's all I could do at that moment. Right before being thrown into the air, I heard the commotion of people attempting to leave in a foreign caravan. Tossed like a courtesan's bed dressings in a Cyrillian brothel. I continued to move through the chaotic crowd of what had once been the Lunamani Festival. Echoed screams resonated in my ears from the mangled bodies within the city. One misplaced step was all it would have taken, just one simple moment of hesitation, and my brief life would have ended in the streets of Fall Lake like the countless others.

As I hurried past a group of mages, a mix of races from Shularix, I saw them giving their all, casting spells at the imminent danger. A ball of fire soared through the air and lit up the dark streets just before smashing into the side of a tailor's workshop. I had been responsible for the construction of Mr. Dowling's shop, and it tugged on my heartstrings to see the damage done to that man's life work. I then turned my glance to a man standing just a few feet away from the blast's impact. The debris was about to topple over onto him. He stood in fear, watching and waiting for his approaching doom. I rushed to him, shouting and waving my hands to get his attention before it was too late.

Or so I thought. He noticed me and ran just in time for the chimney to collapse behind him.

I continued forward on my path towards a blackened void of the unknown. A mother sheltering over her two young children caught my attention and pulled me back into this blood-borne reality. I recognized her. With her husband's recent passing, they would soon relocate to Riversend to live with her mother just north.

Overlapped shouting brought a potential escape at the docks for civilians and visitors alike. Further commands were given to the castle or even to the docks. Others were shouting to take arms, but with a monstrosity this size, nothing appeared to even dent the scales of the colossal abomination or delay its inevitable path of destruction.

"Damn the Draconis. This Draconic horror is almost otherworldly. Is this the moment I am forgotten about in this land? Never found my genuine passion or purpose. Is this truly the life I have desired to live for myself?" I kept asking myself over and over in my unsettled mind.

Cries of desperation were enough to pull my focus back into the danger around me and the occupants of Fall Lake. The same children, pleading for their lives, begged their mother to keep them safe. The children barely had an opportunity to find passion or purpose in their lives. That could not be the end of their young lives. With a quick yet careful push through the crowd, I made my way to the woman and her children. The quaking stomps of the beast as it quickly approached told me there was not much time before its path would fall upon this street. So, I could not let those young lives fall victim to that.

"Come with me. I will find you refuge." The tear-stricken woman ushered her children along behind me as her little boy named Jaxon gripped my finger as tightly as he could to ensure I would never let him go. Her

gaze seemed never to want to be pried from the beast, so I held out my free hand to scoop hers into mine. "Have hope, Milady. Stay strong for the young ones here and have hope. All is not lost. Sir Seig is with you. His protection will keep you all safe." I continued to lead them down a different path, a passage between the walls of the city's second gate.

It seemed I would not make it to my hut at the top of the hill at this point. But I knew of a bunker, a safe place she and her young could hide until, hopefully, the danger had passed. I helped build it. Hell, I helped build much of this city's newest locations over recent years. I knew its workings, and if there was one place to call safe, this may be one of the few locations. So I took them there.

What seemed like an eternity was just mere moments. The sound of the monster's roar rang through my ears, deafening me. At least I believed it was from the beast. There was a sudden pause in sounds as I was leaving the mother and children, with some others taking refuge in the bunker. A flash of a blue light appeared in my eyes. I shook it off. It must have been from the mana usage of the mages I passed before. Or was my mind losing itself?

"You shall be safe here. Have hope, everyone, this is a burden we all share." That was all I remembered saying to everyone as they looked at me just before I shut the bunker door. Leaving the bunker, I made my way back towards my original destination. The mother and her children thanking me profusely and begging me to come with them was a scene that forever made its mark in my memory. It was not fair to these children that they should fall victim to a war they held no action in. Perhaps not following them will be my downfall, the end of my story. I told them to stay safe and live their lives to the fullest before departing the bunker. I stood near a nearby statue and looked up towards the Draconis. The beast showed no sign of slowing down. Its rampage, if anything, had hastened as if every bit of flesh, stone, and dirt it ate was fueling the fires within itself. Like an unstoppable, bloodthirsty machine.

I noticed others making their way up the hill towards the top of the city, where my modest home is situated. The beast had made its way further into the city. Echoes of the insufficient weapons clanging against the creature's impenetrable hide, the smell of the metal and blood in the air. Nothing appeared to penetrate or slow it...

By the time I made it up the hill, I saw worrisome eyes meeting mine as they tried to hide. Hoping their stealth would hide them from the monster's path, my eyes caught one man whom I will never forget. Emptiness and despair filled his eyes while his words spoke of a simple prayer to his deity. His tunic held a holy symbol centered on his chest. A false hope, clinging to their faith that something greater awaits them in the next life. I am not the one to judge them, but I couldn't watch them waiting to be slaughtered. I yelled out to them, encouraging words to give them the courage to get further away. There was another exit that I knew of. Pointing and ushering them to the quickest route out of the city. To this day, I do not know if they took the route or lived, but I showed them a hopeful escape. It was better than listening to their cries and prayers and watching them suffer upon its arrival.

I made my way to my home, continuing to aid and guide others in a last-ditch effort to save their lives. I still don't know why I went there, or what I was going to do, but I allowed my gut to take me home one last time. An enormous sigh escaped me once the creaking door was shut. While resting my back on it, I saw what appeared to be a small fox. No, it was another flash of blue, or was that red? At the time, I was not certain, but a silent ring filled my ears, drowning out the dreadful sounds outside. Picking up the smell of thick blood in the air brought everything back into focus. So much was spilled this day that I could almost taste the metallic flavor on my tongue.

Another massive roar gave me the indication that it was much closer to me now. I shook my head to gather my senses, frantically looking around the plain and mostly empty space I called my home for anything that may help others. "Why have we been damned by the Draconis? There must be something that can be done to calm its rampage, to bring an end to this." Just then, another flash of blue filled my eyes, passing sight of that foxlike creature as my eyes lost vision once again.

Despite the sound of the deafening roar, my ears filled with voices, chants, melodies, songs, and gospels. Languages, both foreign and familiar, overlapped one another like an orchestra playing towards a conjoined connotation. All those people were using their last moments for prayer, in a simple hope that their god answers their call. The sounds pounded through my head over and over like a carpenter's nail. "Does this make them happy? Did it give their last moments purpose? No... I think I get it..." I said to myself before shaking a blue light from my eyes. When I closed them, a glimpse of the people that I had helped on my path here became a beckoning light during moments of despair. It was not just purpose. It was.

Hope.

The idea came to me through the struggles we face today. We fight to bring a better and brighter tomorrow. That we can find a light even in the darkest of days. Strength, passion, unity, faith, and love all start with hope... the vision of those people turned back into a blue light. For once in my life, I think I had found a purpose. With faster movements than I could ever recall in my life, I swung the door wide open. Death, destruction, and a million other descriptions of the massacre await me outside. Returning cries, screams, and pleas for hope returned to my lightly ringing ears. Those people needed something or someone to show them a sign of hope.

I thought I had lost my mind during that moment, to have any inclination that I could do something against that massive beast. Once again, that foxlike creature came into view, its movements leaving a trail of blue light along the ground as it sprinted off. I didn't understand what it was trying to do. Whatever it was, I think it wanted me to follow it. I decided to take my chances on the lost mind I now carry. A tower stood at a close distance and along the fox's path, a favored spot of mine, that overlooked the city and water's edge of Fall Lake. After climbing to the top, I looked at the surrounding people. I did not know the words that I was saying... I almost did not even feel like myself. I felt different. I do not even know how to explain it. It is like my body knows what it needs to do on its own. Telling me to go to this tower, I feel drawn to it. I gave a quick shout

out to them just before a shock hit my hand, causing another flash of blue essence in my eyes. I felt a sense of energy shooting towards me. Of course, the Draconis monster, but I believed it to be something else...

The people moved as I shouted protective commands at them. Again, the words just flowed from my lips. They tried to find shelter and a way out of the beast's path, but for me, that light was the path of hope I followed. I had hope. An ideal, at least in whatever I did next. I moved with greater strides and a purpose to find whatever awaited me at the top of the tower. My feet moved faster than I believed to be humanly possible. The quakes of the stairs beneath my feet told me the creature was almost there. Drawing closer to my end, I climbed that tower faster. But something about me was different...

I stood at the top of that tower with pride, even if it was to look out onto the beautiful city one last time to watch the glistening sunset across the clear blue waters of the lake. Again, another light, the foxlike creature was absent from my view, nowhere to be seen around me. I saw a flash of blue and red pulse outward. My eyes deceived me as I saw the city in its highest glory. Beautiful architecture going on for miles, blue tinted walls surrounding it in its entirety. A large and exquisite castle sitting atop a neighboring hill. I glanced around to see myself standing on a balcony, no larger than the tower I stood on at that moment. I appeared to be looking out to the lake once again, but the location seemed foreign. The blood, death, torment, and the unholy living weapon that just moments prior was laying waste to the land was all gone. That... was hope, a grand view of the brightest light of tomorrow that could be born from the darkness of despair today. I felt something brush against my leg. The foxlike creature had returned. Its touch was comforting and familiar to me, but within a moment, it disappeared along with the vision.

It all made sense to me at that moment. I did not know how, but I felt the need to want to do something, so I told myself that I would. I needed to deal with this threat, but I was just Arlo Devine. What could I have done? I felt something in my hands, a blue spark coursing through them, encircled by a white mist of energy. Was that Mana? What was happening to me? I heard something, a voice. It was soothing, and echoed through my core, somehow filling a part of the void I felt deprived of in my life. It sounded as if it came from the sky. My eyes flashed with blue light and instantly storm clouds appeared, hiding the eclipsed twin moons within the evening sky. I instinctively turned to the path the beast carved on its way directly up the hill and straight towards me. I held no fear in my heart and mind. A quick glance at my hands once again I appeared to be encompassed in this blue and white light. Sparks continued to form and branch up my arms until I became a living conduit of lightning. I heard voices, visions flashed once again before my eyes of people and their last hopes as they began to fade away from this world. No, they were not fading away. They were the surrounding energy that encompassed me. The beast finally approached, trampling and stomping upon anything and anyone it could. We were all mere ants in comparison to its gargantuan size. I put pressure onto my bent legs, leaning into it and readying myself. Ready to pounce as the hunter, awaiting the opportune moments to strike its prey. The voice spoke to me again. I spoke the same words aloud to let the two voices overlap.

"I have Hope."

My eyes saw everything more clearly in that moment. The buildings, the bodies, the crops, the animals, all left in a wake of despair behind it. I was only Arlo Devine, a man who until that day had lacked a purpose in life, no real thing to truly be passionate about, just a man who worked day and night, giving everything he could for others and taking little in regards for himself. I found hope in those moments, a hope that even if I could not stop the beast. My efforts would delay it so that others would not suffer the same end. Pressing from the stone tower I found myself launched into the air, the tower's stone foundation was crumbling from the leap that propelled me forward. Time seemed to slow, a monstrous abomination of Draconis descent scaled, strong, and invulnerable. Flashes of my life clouded my vision and my slowed ascent into the sky above. My scream echoed throughout the entire city like howling thunder that rivaled the roar of the beast itself. Cracks of lightning struck around the city. My hand reared back high above my head, outstretched completely. I held the weapon of Hope, and I was ready to smite this damned creature that brought darkness upon all these lives. If that is what it takes, then my life for yours. Cobalt energy filled my hands. Closing my hand around it into a fist ready to strike the beast. My eyes covered and lost again behind the blue and white. The last thing I witnessed was the muzzle of this monstrosity, the swirling void of chaos and destruction within its reptilian eyes. Then silence. Blue light. Emptiness. This must be the serenity of death. To wade in the void of nothingness, lost in maddening thought for the rest of eternity. I felt like I was lying in a shallow pool of water, hopeful that my actions were not in vain, and that I could find acceptance in my fate. I had hoped that all would be well, even if my life was only able to save those who remained in the city. More visions flashed over my eyes, things that had been, that were, and what could be. But these were not dreams of my life.

They were the lives of others.

Finally, sound had returned to my ears, or perhaps they were noises in my mind to break the madness that I had fallen to. The sounds were too hard for me to comprehend exactly what they were. At times they came as voices, of strange dialect I have never heard in my life. Some were yelling, others crying, and a few laughing. I then felt a jerk as metal clanged in my head and echoed into an ear-splitting headache. The sound was familiar, hammer hitting metal within a forge, or two warriors engaged in combat, parrying the blows of their iron swords. Swirling sounds of speed, flame and chaotic energy of magic whisked through the air once again. My nostrils filled with a metallic smell, the flavor of blood on my tongue. Echoing voices of the Hopeful, reverberated in my ear.

Then all went silent once again.

The silence was lonesome. The voices I had been hearing at least gave comfort, giving me an illusion that I was not alone in this abyss. But I soon came to the realization that they were gone. I tried to open my eyes as I heard shouting again, the blue in my vision moving in unidentifiable shapes. All I could see was the black emptiness, as the blue light moved towards where my hands should have been. Mixing with the white and formed into the long shape of a road, I heard a tingling in my hand, what sounded like my voice speaking to me, while the energy of blue and white pulsed with every syllable.

If you have hope for a brighter tomorrow. Stand tall and take hope into your own hands. Accept their pain as your own and share hope's light with the world.

I did the only thing I knew how to do. Find hope within despair, and I tightened my hands, gripping upon what appeared to be within my reach. And as I grasped the light, feeling its energy course through my body, and then outward from my body as if I was the conduit for the lightning. Ringing filled my ears from a massive thunderous crack and the weight of something massive falling from the strength of hope in my hands. My eyes fell victim to the deep blue light, and all plunged into absolute silence.

Burdens of Hope
A Companion Novella of The Hopebringer Trilogy
Within the collection of the Legends of Lyorion Series
ISBN (Paperback): 979-8-9945420-1-9
First Edition: 2026
Printed in the United States of America

www.uglymunkey.com

Artwork by @d0za.art on Instagram.

A special thank you to anyone who chooses to carry *Hope* forward.

www.ingramcontent.com/pod-product-compliance
Lightning Source LLC
LaVergne TN
LVHW040223110826
845146LV00004B/1271

9798994542019